Hello, Stanford Tree!

Aimee Aryal

Illustrated by Brad Alston

MASCOT BOOKS
www.mascotbooks.com

It was a beautiful fall day in Palo Alto. The Stanford Tree was on his way to Stanford Stadium for a football game. The mascot started his journey on the Main Quad.

Students on the quad were
thrilled to see the Stanford Tree.
They cheered, "Hello, Stanford Tree!"

The Stanford Tree walked in
front of Stanford Memorial Church.
The mascot said a prayer for the
Cardinal before continuing his journey.

Outside the church, he ran
into more Stanford fans. The fans
hollered, "Hello, Stanford Tree!"

The Stanford Tree continued to the Stanford Mausoleum. He admired the beautiful structure and noticed the sphinxes at the entrance.

A professor walking by
noticed the mascot and called,
"Hello, Stanford Tree!"

The tree's next stop was the
famous Hoover Tower. At the tower,
the mascot ran into Stanford fans
on their way to the big game.

The mascot made the fans laugh with his antics. The fans called, "Go, Cardinal!"

The Stanford Tree's next
stop was Green Library. The
mascot returned a library book
before continuing his journey.

Outside the library, the tree
came across more students. Happy
to see the mascot, the students
cheered, "Hello, Stanford Tree!"

At Maples Pavilion, the Stanford Tree played basketball. Two basketball coaches spotted the mascot and said, "Nice shot, Stanford Tree!"

The mascot was excited for the upcoming basketball season, but first he had a job to do at the football stadium.

Finally, the Stanford Tree
arrived at Stanford Stadium. In
front of the stadium, the mascot
ran into Cardinal fans.

Everyone was excited to
see the Stanford Tree. They
cheered, "Hello, Stanford Tree!"

The Stanford Tree joined
the football team as they made
their way onto the football field.

Fans cheered the team's
arrival. They cheered,
"Let's go, Cardinal!"

The Stanford Tree watched
the game from the sidelines and
cheered for the home team.

The wide receiver made
a beautiful catch in the endzone.
"Touchdown, Stanford Tree!"
called the quarterback.

At halftime, the Stanford Tree led the Leland Stanford Junior University Marching Band onto the field.

With the mascot conducting,
the band played "Come Join The Band"
to the delight of Stanford fans.

With great play, the Stanford
Cardinal won the football game.
The team celebrated by dumping
water on the coach.

The coach said, "Great game, team! Thank you for your support, Stanford Tree!"

After the game, the Stanford Tree
made his way home through the
Rodin Sculpture Garden.

Finally, the mascot was back home and in his cozy bed. As he drifted to sleep, he thought about what a great day he had at Stanford University.

Good night, Stanford Tree.

For Anna and Maya. ~ Aimee Aryal

For more information about our products,
please visit us online at www.mascotbooks.com.

For more information, please contact Mascot Books,
P.O. Box 220157, Chantilly, VA 20153-0157

ISBN: 1-934878-67-5

PRT0909A

Printed in the United States.

www.mascotbooks.com

aseball

Team	Title	Author
oston Red Sox	Hello, *Wally*!	Jerry Remy
oston Red Sox	*Wally The Green Monster* And His Journey Through *Red Sox Nation*!	Jerry Remy
oston Red Sox	Coast to Coast with *Wally The Green Monster*	Jerry Remy
oston Red Sox	A Season with *Wally The Green Monster*	Jerry Remy
oston Red Sox	*Wally' The Green Monster And His* World Tour	Jerry Remy
Chicago Cubs	Let's Go, *Cubs*!	Aimee Aryal
Chicago White Sox	Let's Go, *White Sox*!	Aimee Aryal
Colorado Rockies	Hello, *Dinger*!	Aimee Aryal
Detroit Tigers	Hello, *Paws*!	Aimee Aryal
LA Angels	Let's Go, *Angels*!	Aimee Aryal
LA Dodgers	Let's Go, *Dodgers*!	Aimee Aryal
Milwaukee Brewers	Hello, *Bernie Brewer*!	Aimee Aryal
New York Yankees	Let's Go, *Yankees*!	Yogi Berra
New York Yankees	*Yankees* Town	Aimee Aryal
New York Mets	Hello, *Mr. Met*!	Rusty Staub
New York Mets	*Mr. Met* and his Journey Through the Big Apple	Aimee Aryal
Oakland Athletics	Let's Go, *A's*!	Aimee Aryal
Philadelphia Phillies	Hello, *Phillie Phanatic*!	Aimee Aryal
Cleveland Indians	Hello, *Slider*!	Bob Feller
San Francisco Giants	Go, *Giants*, Go!	Aimee Aryal
Seattle Mariners	Hello, *Mariner Moose*!	Aimee Aryal
St. Louis Cardinals	Hello, *Fredbird*!	Ozzie Smith
Washington Nationals	Hello, *Screech*!	Aimee Aryal

Pro Football

Team	Title	Author
Carolina Panthers	Let's Go, Panthers!	Aimee Aryal
Chicago Bears	Let's Go, Bears!	Aimee Aryal
Dallas Cowboys	How 'Bout Them Cowboys!	Aimee Aryal
Green Bay Packers	Go, Pack, Go!	Aimee Aryal
Kansas City Chiefs	Let's Go, Chiefs!	Aimee Aryal
Minnesota Vikings	Let's Go, Vikings!	Aimee Aryal
New York Giants	Let's Go, Giants!	Aimee Aryal
New York Jets	J-E-T-S! Jets, Jets, Jets!	Aimee Aryal
New England Patriots	Let's Go, Patriots!	Aimee Aryal
Pittsburg Steelers	Here We Go, Steelers!	Aimee Aryal
Seattle Seahawks	Let's Go, Seahawks!	Aimee Aryal

Basketball

Team	Title	Author
Dallas Mavericks	Let's Go, Mavs!	Mark Cuban
Boston Celtics	Let's Go, Celtics!	Aimee Aryal

Other

	Title	Author
National	Bo America's Commander In Leash	Naren Aryal
Kentucky Derby	White Diamond Runs For The Roses	Aimee Aryal
Marine Corps Marathon	Run, Miles, Run!	Aimee Aryal

College

School	Title	Author
Alabama	Hello, Big Al!	Aimee Aryal
Alabama	Roll Tide!	Ken Stabler
Alabama	Big Al's Journey Through the Yellowhammer State	Aimee Aryal
Arizona	Hello, Wilbur!	Lute Olson
Arizona State	Hello, Sparky!	Aimee Aryal
Arkansas	Hello, Big Red!	Aimee Aryal
Arkansas	Big Red's Journey Through the Razorback State	Aimee Aryal
Auburn	Hello, Aubie!	Aimee Aryal
Auburn	War Eagle!	Pat Dye
Auburn	Aubie's Journey Through the Yellowhammer State	Aimee Aryal
Boston College	Hello, Baldwin!	Aimee Aryal
Brigham Young	Hello, Cosmo!	LaVell Edwards
Cal - Berkeley	Hello, Oski!	Aimee Aryal
Cincinnati	Hello, Bearcat!	Mick Cronin
Clemson	Hello, Tiger!	Aimee Aryal
Clemson	Tiger's Journey Through the Palmetto State	Aimee Aryal
Colorado	Hello, Ralphie!	Aimee Aryal
Connecticut	Hello, Jonathan!	Aimee Aryal
Duke	Hello, Blue Devil!	Aimee Aryal
Florida	Hello, Albert!	Aimee Aryal
Florida	Albert's Journey Through the Sunshine State	Aimee Aryal
Florida State	Let's Go, 'Noles!	Aimee Aryal
Georgia	Hello, Hairy Dawg!	Aimee Aryal
Georgia	How 'Bout Them Dawgs!	Vince Dooley
Georgia	Hairy Dawg's Journey Through the Peach State	Vince Dooley
Georgia Tech	Hello, Buzz!	Aimee Aryal
Gonzaga	Spike, The Gonzaga Bulldog	Mike Pringle
Illinois	Let's Go, Illini!	Aimee Aryal
Indiana	Let's Go, Hoosiers!	Aimee Aryal
Iowa	Hello, Herky!	Aimee Aryal
Iowa State	Hello, Cy!	Amy DeLashmutt
James Madison	Hello, Duke Dog!	Aimee Aryal
Kansas	Hello, Big Jay!	Aimee Aryal
Kansas	Hello, Willie!	Dan Walter
Kansas State	Willie the Wildcat's Journey Through the Sunflower State	Dan Walter
Kentucky	Hello, Wildcat!	Aimee Aryal
LSU	Hello, Mike!	Aimee Aryal
LSU	Mike's Journey Through the Bayou State	Aimee Aryal
Maryland	Hello, Testudo!	Aimee Aryal
Michigan	Let's Go, Blue!	Aimee Aryal
Michigan State	Hello, Sparty!	Aimee Aryal
Michigan State	Sparty's Journey Through Michigan	Aimee Aryal
Middle Tennessee	Hello, Lightning!	Aimee Aryal
Minnesota	Hello, Goldy!	Aimee Aryal
Mississippi	Hello, Colonel Rebel!	Aimee Aryal
Mississippi State	Hello, Bully!	Aimee Aryal
Missouri	Hello, Truman!	Todd Donoho
Missouri	Hello, Truman! Show Me Missouri!	Todd Donoho
Nebraska	Hello, Herbie Husker!	Aimee Aryal
North Carolina	Hello, Rameses!	Aimee Aryal
North Carolina	Rameses' Journey Through the Tar Heel State	Aimee Aryal
North Carolina St.	Hello, Mr. Wuf!	Aimee Aryal
North Carolina St.	Mr. Wuf's Journey Through North Carolina	Aimee Aryal
Northern Arizona	Hello, Louie!	Jeanette Baker
Notre Dame	Let's Go, Irish!	Aimee Aryal
Ohio State	Hello, Brutus!	Aimee Aryal
Ohio State	Brutus' Journey	Aimee Aryal
Oakland	Hello, Grizz!	Dawn Aubry
Oklahoma	Let's Go, Sooners!	Aimee Aryal
Oklahoma State	Hello, Pistol Pete!	Aimee Aryal
Oregon	Go Ducks!	Aimee Aryal
Oregon State	Hello, Benny the Beaver!	Aimee Aryal
Penn State	Hello, Nittany Lion!	Aimee Aryal
Penn State	We Are Penn State!	Joe Paterno
Purdue	Hello, Purdue Pete!	Aimee Aryal
Rutgers	Hello, Scarlet Knight!	Aimee Aryal
South Carolina	Hello, Cocky!	Aimee Aryal
South Carolina	Cocky's Journey Through the Palmetto State	Aimee Aryal
So. California	Hello, Tommy Trojan!	Aimee Aryal
Syracuse	Hello, Otto!	Aimee Aryal
Tennessee	Hello, Smokey!	Aimee Aryal
Tennessee	Smokey's Journey Through the Volunteer State	Aimee Aryal
Texas	Hello, Hook 'Em!	Aimee Aryal
Texas	Hook 'Em's Journey Through the Lone Star State	Aimee Aryal
Texas A & M	Howdy, Reveille!	Aimee Aryal
Texas A & M	Reveille's Journey Through the Lone Star State	Aimee Aryal
Texas Tech	Hello, Masked Rider!	Aimee Aryal
UCLA	Hello, Joe Bruin!	Aimee Aryal
Virginia	Hello, CavMan!	Aimee Aryal
Virginia Tech	Hello, Hokie Bird!	Aimee Aryal
Virginia Tech	Yea, It's Hokie Game Day!	Frank Beamer
Virginia Tech	Hokie Bird's Journey Through Virginia	Aimee Aryal
Wake Forest	Hello, Demon Deacon!	Aimee Aryal
Washington	Hello, Harry the Husky!	Aimee Aryal
Washington State	Hello, Butch!	Aimee Aryal
West Virginia	Hello, Mountaineer!	Aimee Aryal
West Virginia	The Mountaineer's Journey Through West Virginia	Leslie H. Haning
Wisconsin	Hello, Bucky!	Aimee Aryal
Wisconsin	Bucky's Journey Through the Badger State	Aimee Aryal

Order online at **mascotbooks.com** using promo code " **free**" to receive **FREE SHIPPING**!

More great titles coming soon!

info@mascotbooks.com

MASCOT BOOKS

www.mascotbooks.com

SCHOOL PROGRAM

Promote reading. Build spirit. Raise money.™

Mascot Books® is creating customized children's books for public and private elementary schools all across America. Containing school-specific story lines and illustrations, our books are beloved by principals, librarians, teachers, parents, and of course, by young readers.

Our books feature your mascot taking a tour of your school, while highlighting all the things and events that make your school community such a special place.

The Mascot Books Elementary School Program is an innovative way to promote reading and build spirit, while offering a fresh, new marketing or fundraising opportunity.

Starting Is As Easy As 1-2-3!

1 You tell us all about your school community. What makes your school unique? What are your well-known traditions? Why do parents and students love your school?

2 With the information you share with us, Mascot Books creates a one-of-a-kind hardcover children's book featuring your school and your mascot.

3 Your book is delivered!

MASCOT BOOKS

www.mascotbooks.com

AUTHORS

If you have a book idea—no matter the subject—we'd like to hear from you.

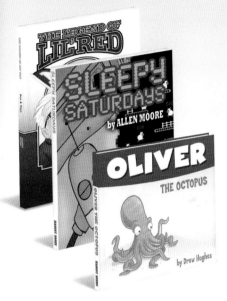

What we do for Mascot Books® Authors

- Review your manuscript
- Character design and concept creation
- Illustrations
- Cover design and book layout
- Book printing
- Sales strategies

Why become a Mascot Books® Author?

- You retain full ownership of your story
- You set your own book price
- Getting a traditional publisher to take interest in your project is nearly impossible, and if they do, they take full control of your book and offer you a small royalty of 7% – 9%

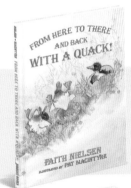

From Here to There and Back With A Quack!
by Faith Nielsen

Little Kay Learns the Golden Rule
by Amir Mostafavi and Roya Mattis

Matt the Bat , Kitt the Mitt , and Paul the Ball
by Jim Rooker